PUDDING BAG SCHOOL

COLD Enough FOR Snow

D1157679

PUDDING BAG SCHOOL

COLD ENOUGH FOR SNOW

Hilary McKay

Illustrated by
David Melling

Hodder
Children's
Books

a division of Hodder Headline Limited

CHAPTER ONE

Dinner Ladies' Detention

On the day that the weather finally became cold enough for snow, Class 4b, Pudding Bag School, were given dinner ladies' detention. Nobody escaped. They had choked too long and too loudly and too disrespectfully on Mock Cod Pie. Mrs Muldoon, the chief dinner lady, had taken their choking for cheek, and reported them to their class teacher.

Miss Gilhoolie, wondering all the time what sort of an animal a Mock Cod might be, suggested tentatively that Class 4b might have choked on the bones.

"There were no bones," said Mrs Muldoon. "It was the finest fillet."

"In a light cheese sauce," chimed in Miss

Spigot, the second dinner lady "With a mashed potato top."

"And ekeing!"

That was Amelia Pilchard, the third and last dinner lady. Mrs Muldoon was large and purple, and Miss Spigot was bony and blue but Amelia Pilchard blended into the landscape like fog. She specialised in the art of ekeing, the mingling of unnatural ingredients with the natural ones, in order to make them go further.

"Perhaps," said Miss Gilhoolie, "it was the ekeing that choked them, poor lambs!"

"There would be no fish pie without ekeing!" Mrs Muldoon told her sternly.

"Best tapioca in a cod's head stock!" said Amelia Pilchard.

"Wouldn't choke a day-old kitten!" said Miss Spigot.

"That choking," said Mrs Muldoon, "was no more or less than out-and-out insolence led by that red-headed Dougal McDougal!"

This sounded more than probable to Miss Gilhoolie, so she said, Well, Poor Dears, Detention it must be, I will let their families know you are keeping them at school.

That was how Class 4b ended up alone in Pudding Bag School with the three dinner ladies when the first snowflake fell.

Nobody noticed it. It drifted down like the ghost of a forgotten thought and vanished before it touched the ground, but it was the first of millions.

Dinner ladies' detention took place in the dining hall, a high-windowed and echoing and very chilly part of the building. Class 4b were given rough paper and pencils and the menu board to copy out fifty times each as punishment, and the dinner ladies retreated to the comparative warmth of the cleaner's cupboard.

Simon Percy, who kept a diary, copied down the menu from the menu board as Madeline Brown read it out.

MOCK COD PIE/ MILD MIXED ROOT
CURRY

RUSSIAN TRIFLE/JELLY SURPRISE
All made from the finest ingredients

"All made from the *same* ingredients!" commented Dougal McDougal. "The only difference between the trifle and the pie was that one had bits of beetroot and the other had bits of fish. And the jelly had beetroot in as well."

"The jelly and the curry were both out the same tin," said Simon Percy. "I saw Miss Spigot scraping it out. Only they hotted it up for the curry. Beetroot, tapioca and mashed potato it was. Lend me a line-writer somebody."

Line-writers had been introduced at Pudding Bag School the previous term. They had been invented by Madeline Brown, the school brain, and manufactured by Mr Bedwig, ex-caretaker. You slid your paper into a wooden frame and a simple mechanism of cogs and levers allowed twenty pencils to be operated at once. Simon was handed half a dozen by people who had already completed their fifty copies of the menu board.

"I do miss Mr Bedwig," remarked Simon, as he set to work, and there was a murmur of agreement from all around. Mr Bedwig had

4

arrived at Pudding Bag School the previous term and no caretaker could have been more useful. He had been just in time to help Class 4b build a rocket that had successfully blasted their frightful headmaster into space. The rocket had been designed by Madeline, but it had been Mr Bedwig who had come by most of the parts and carried out the actual welding. Also, he had located Simon Percy's long-lost parents, redecorated the entire school, installed solar panels on the roof and an escape tunnel in the basement, banished chewing gum from the premises, and adopted a cat. Then, when everything was back to normal and everyone just settling down to live happily ever after he had announced that he was needed elsewhere, and vanished without trace.

"At least he left the cat," said Madeline. The cat, Bagdemagus, was curled up on her lap. He was the warmest thing in the school. "I wonder . . ."

Right in the middle of Madeline's wonder the dining hall door was pushed open and Kate McDougal, Dougal's seventeen-year-old sister, blew into the room, white from head to foot and radiating cold and excitement. Dougal had seven older sisters, but Kate, as well as being the youngest and prettiest and kindest, was by far the most excitable.

"Such snow!" she exclaimed, shaking clouds of it from her hair as she spoke. "What are you all doing, still at school? Darling Dougal, I brought your wellies! Hadn't you better come home straight away?"

"Snow!" shrieked Class 4b in delight, and there was an immediate rush to the windows.

"Up to my knees," Kate told them. "And drifting already. Didn't you notice?"

"No," said Dougal. "We've been doing dinner ladies' detention. We can't go home yet either, we've got another half hour."

"Dinner ladies are ogres," said Kate dispassionately. "What are they making you do?"

"Write out the menu fifty times each. Nobody minds very much. We've been using Mr Bedwig's line-writing machines."

"Mr Bedwig was a poppet," remarked Kate, perching herself on a windowsill and

swinging her legs. "I wonder how he's getting on at the zoo."

Line-writing, dinner ladies and even the knee-high snow outside were forgotten in the buzz of excitement that followed.

"What's he doing at the zoo?"

"Caretaking of course."

"How do you know?"

"I saw him."

"Why didn't you tell anyone?"

"I didn't think," said Kate. "I didn't know you didn't know. I saw him when I went to say goodbye."

"To Mr Bedwig?"

"To the animals. They're being moved. Sent home most of them. Not the cold weather ones."

"But why?"

"Because of the weather forecast," explained Kate patiently. "You know. Flooding. Arctic freezes. Lots of snow. They've been saying it all winter."

"It never comes, though."

"It's here now," said Kate cheerfully. "Just look at it out there! Coming down in bucketfuls! And the Thames burst its banks this morning. Solid ice, South London is, all the way to Kent!"

For weeks and weeks this sort of weather had been forecast. People had laid in huge supplies of food and books and candles and board games to amuse the children in the event of power cuts. Travel agents had made fortunes selling holidays in the winter sun. Knitted underwear had come back into fashion, along with thermal vests, paraffin stoves and family sing-songs round pots of lentil soup. Then December had passed and been the mildest on record and people, after all their preparations, began to feel a little foolish. January was the first frost-free January in living memory. The weather forecasters should be sacked, people said, spreading rumours like that.

In the first week of February the daffodils came out and were washed away by six months' supply of rain falling in two days.

"I suppose it was the rain that spoilt all the poor daffodils that caused these floods," said Kate.

"I suppose it was," agreed Madeline thoughtfully, with her nose pressed to the window.

"And now this!"

"At last!" rejoiced Dougal. "We've never had real proper snow before."

A gust of wind hit the window so hard that it burst open. Blinding whiteness filled the room, every piece of paper went flying, aching cold attacked from all sides and a deep howling echoed through the hall. It took half a dozen people to push the window shut again, and then the white cloud cleared and the howling diminished and Class 4b were left staring at each other in shocked amazement.

"Good job I brought your wellies," said Kate to Dougal, but she sounded a little uncertain as she said it. It was not like Kate to be pessimistic, but she could not help wondering if wellies would be enough to ensure that Dougal got safely home that night. And even if they were, worried Kate, what about the rest of Class 4b, wellieless, and many of them considerably smaller and less robust than her brother.

Madeline answered her unspoken thought.

"We shan't get home in that," said Madeline.

The noise when the dining hall window blew open had penetrated even to the cleaners' cupboard.

"How those kiddies do howl!" remarked Miss Spigot, as she dunked her sixth custard cream in her mug of ovaltine.

"Stomach ache," said Mrs Muldoon wisely. "Martyrs to it, children are. Mine were all the same."

Amelia Pilchard tittered silently.

"All six," continued Mrs Muldoon. "Terrible groaners, till the end."

"The end?" queried Miss Spigot softly, sensing tragedy.

"Took off," said Mrs Muldoon, not softly at all, and there was a general tutting of disappointment and disapproval in the cleaning cupboard.

"Never wrote?" asked Miss Spigot, after a suitable pause.

"Not a line."

"Boys, I suppose."

"Boys *and* girls," replied Mrs Muldoon after some thought. "Four and two. More or less. There's no gratitude in this world for those that bring up children."

There was a lot of solemn nodding in the cupboard. It was getting very warm by this time, the dinner ladies having built up between them quite a cosy fug. The sounds from the dining hall had died away with the closing of the window and there was nothing to be heard but the shuffle of biscuits in the biscuit tin as Amelia Pilchard poked through the top layers in search of the broken fragments underneath.

"There's no gratitude in the world *at all*, if you ask me," remarked Miss Spigot. "Look at us! Where would they be without us dinner ladies, and yet never a word of thanks!"

"We should get medals!"

"Honoured by the nation!"

"OBEs."

"There's been dinner ladies done it."

"I should just fancy being a dame," said Mrs Muldoon dreamily.

"Dame Lacie Muldoon!"

"Dame Pansy Spigot!"

"Dame Amelia Pilchard!"

They sighed with bliss and reached again for the biscuit tin.

"I wonder if those dinner ladies of yours know about this weather," said Kate suddenly. "I'm going to find them!" And she went and hammered on the cleaning cupboard door.

The dinner ladies were terribly concerned when they heard about the snow. They peered out of the windows trying to see through the swarming whiteness outside, and flinched as the glass shook and rattled in the gale. They looked at each other, and then they looked at Class 4b and they said almost exactly what Madeline had said earlier.

"They'll never get home in that!"

"You might," said Kate, and this was true. Mrs Muldoon with her bulk and her zip-up fleece-lined boots might make it home. So might Miss Spigot, built as she was like animated scaffolding. So might Amelia

14

Pilchard, whose soupy exterior concealed a constitution of enormous toughness, but . . .

"Leave the kiddies!" cried Miss Spigot. "Never!"

"Here we stay," agreed Miss Pilchard.

"Like it or lump it," said Mrs Muldoon. "Still, we can put it down as overtime. *And* unsociable hours. *Very* unsociable hours!"

Then for the first time it dawned on Class 4b that they were there for the night. Stuck in Pudding Bag School in the middle of a blizzard with the three dinner ladies for comfort. Samantha Freebody burst into tears, Emma and Charlotte, the identical twins, began identical hysterics, and several people began to groan.

"Stop it, please stop it!" begged Kate, with her hands over her ears. "It might not even be for all night. The snow could stop any minute."

"It's up to the windowsills now," said Simon.

"I'm terribly hungry," said Dougal McDougal, and immediately wished he hadn't because the dinner ladies looked at each other and said, "Supper!"

"Darling Mrs Muldoon," said Kate. "Don't bother about supper!" But neither Mrs Muldoon nor her assistants would hear of not bothering. They said cooking was their duty, and cook they would. They said it would be a disgrace if they didn't. They grew quite excited at the thought. There was not much in, they said, but nothing to stop them having a rake around.

"Soup," said Miss Pilchard. "Soup's a treat for ekeing."

"Dumplings in it," said Miss Spigot. "All kiddies love dumplings."

"Hot milk and bicarb," said Mrs Muldoon. "All my six had hot milk and bicarb at bedtime. Sent them off proper!"

Inspired and self righteous, wreathed in charitable smiles, they nudged each other and departed.

"Who would have thought they would be so kind?" exclaimed Kate, not knowing the little song that was already beginning in each dinner lady's head.

"Dame Lacie Muldoon!"

"Dame Pansy Spigot!"

"Dame Amelia Pilchard!"

"Kind!" groaned Dougal, when the dinner ladies had gone. "You won't say that when you taste their cooking! I'm not sure I can bear it twice in one day, and we've already eaten Mock Cod Pie."

"If we are going to sleep here," said Simon Percy, "*where* are we going to sleep? Not in the dining hall?"

"Nor with the dinner ladies," said Dougal McDougal.

"No, no," agreed everyone at once. "*Definitely* not with the dinner ladies!"

In the kitchen an identical discussion was taking place. "Definitely not with the kiddies!" called Miss Spigot through clouds of steam, and Mrs Muldoon and Amelia Pilchard nodded in agreement.

"Cooking, yes," stated Mrs Muldoon ponderously. "That I will undertake. Cossetting, no! And sleeping with the little horro . . . dears I would regard as cossetting. They will be up and down all night, and there would not be a minute's peace. Besides, they won't be alone. They've got Young Kate. How's the soup Amelia, dear?"

"Thickening beautifully," crooned Amelia Pilchard, scooping dollops of mashed potato into a simmering vat of tap water. "Time for the dumplings!"

"Lovely, lovely dumplings!" sang Miss Spigot as she swayed across the kitchen with an enormous trayful of floury balls that shone with a pale and greenish light.

"Parsley?" enquired Mrs Muldoon.

"That cabbage they never ate Thursday," Miss Spigot told her complacently.

"Tuesday," said Miss Pilchard.

"Tuesday then. Chopped it up and popped it in. Waste not, want not."

"Set 'em up beautiful for the night," said Mrs Muldoon cheerfully. "And as for us, I thought we might tuck up in here. Leave on the gas oven and fetch in the staff room armchairs."

"Borrow the Infants' telly and make a pot of tea," suggested Miss Spigot. "Tea-leaf fortunes we could have. Amelia does them a treat! Got a real gift, our Amelia."

"I see us all kneeling," murmured Amelia, stirring the soup with her eyes half closed. "In a big, big room. Flags dangling from the ceiling and purple cushions and a person in a knobbly gold hat . . ."

Class 4b spent the night in their classroom for want of anywhere better. They moved the chairs and tables to make a space in the middle, piled the dressing up clothes into a heap, and lay down on top of it under a

layer of coats. Then each of them tried with desperate earnestness not to think of potato soup and cabbage dumplings. The hot milk flavoured with bicarbonate of soda had been nothing in comparison.

At first it was very cold and draughty, but towards the end of the night it grew noticeably warmer. The windowpanes rattled less and less and then stopped. The howl of the wind became a muffled roar and then a gentle murmur.

Madeline Brown woke from a dream of summer and realised that it was morning. The classroom was almost dark but the tops of the windows showed a line of pale light. All around her Class 4b lay sprawled and sighing on piles of old clothes, reminding her of left-over jumble from a jumble sale. There was a distant humming in the air like the sound of the summer bees in her dream.

CHAPTER TWO

Snow up to the Windows

After Madeline, Samantha Freebody was the next to wake. She rubbed her eyes and scratched her neck and stared confusedly round the room.

"Hello," whispered Madeline.

"Oh!" said Samantha. "Oh Madeline! What did we . . . ? Why are we . . . ?"

"Snow," Madeline reminded her.

"Oh yes! Oh no! Oh Madeline!"

Samantha, gradually wakening up, was beginning to understand. The darkness and the muffled sound from outside and the lack of draughts.

"The snow's up to the windows now, isn't it?" she asked.

Madeline nodded.

"Nearly over them?"

Madeline nodded again.

Snow up to the windows, wrote Simon Percy in his diary, making it official.

On the whole there was very little panic. People were alarmed but also rather excited. Class 4b were not unused to adventures. After all, they reminded each other, they had faced difficulties in the past and (helped by some remarkable good luck) overcome them most successfully. Only the twins were truly frightened. Charlotte and Emma were new that term, and never, they whimpered between chattering teeth, had they had to deal with people as alarming as the Pudding Bag School dinner ladies. ("You ought to have seen our old headmaster!" people told them at this announcement. "Coo gosh!")

Nor, said Charlotte and Emma, interrupting the eager descriptions of the old headmaster that were beginning on all sides, had they ever before spent a single night away from Mummy and Daddy. ("S'nothing," said Simon Percy comfortingly.

"My parents were away for ten years!")

Charlotte and Emma looked at him in disbelief.

"It's perfectly true," said Dougal McDougal. "They went off in a hot air balloon."

"Our family never do things like that," said Emma thankfully, and in response to the questions of their classmates, the twins also admitted that they had never once done anything even slightly original . . .

("You should have seen the rocket we built!" said Samuel Moon).

Or exciting . . .

("You should have seen it going *up*!" said Dougal).

Or dangerous . . .

("You should have been *on it*!" said Madeline.)

"Madeline had to parachute down," Samuel told the twins.

"Anyway," said Simon Percy. "It's not as if we were stuck here by ourselves. We've got Kate. You're practically grown up, aren't you Kate?"

"Oh, practically," agreed Kate cheerfully

as she climbed onto a desk to try and peer through the top of the windows. "What *is* that funny humming noise?"

The dinner ladies (being unable to get the Infants' television to work) had gone to bed early and spent a cosy night on two armchairs each in front of the open oven door. Morning came as a horrible shock to them.

"It's never gone and snowed all night has it?" demanded Mrs Muldoon.

"I'm afraid it has," said Miss Pilchard. She had been the first to wake and had had time to work out the situation.

"Don't tell me we'll be stuck with them kiddies *again*," groaned Miss Spigot.

"I'm afraid we will."

"After what we did last night I was planning to put in for my Damehood today," grumbled Mrs Muldoon. "I thought I'd try Downing Street."

"I thought I'd try the Palace," said Miss Spigot.

"I thought I'd try the phones again," said Amelia Pilchard. "See if they'd repaired them since last night, but they're still dead this morning. And the telly's dead. And the lights keep flickering and the heating's off and the children's awake!"

Strangely, Miss Pilchard's list of bad news brought out the best in the dinner ladies. They pulled themselves out of their armchairs and began to tackle the problem of breakfast.

"Which is no joke," said Mrs Muldoon. "Being as there was no deliveries yesterday, nor will be today and we don't keep in hardly any stores except for the Emergency Freezer."

The Emergency Freezer was where odds and ends of past school dinners were kept.

"But we shall need what's in there for ourselves," said Mrs Muldoon. "We shan't want to squander it on the children. Make us some toast, Pansy dear, while we have a little think."

Tapioca and toast crust porridge was the result of the dinner ladies' little think. The twins almost started weeping again at the sight of it, but Madeline courageously began hers at once.

"That's right!" said Kate. "Come on twins!

Close your eyes and get it over with! Scrape your plates everyone! I expect it will only come back hotted up for lunch if you don't!"

Mrs Muldoon, returning a few minutes later to see how they were enjoying their breakfast, was surprised and gratified at the sight of so many empty plates.

"Eaten the lot!" she announced triumphantly to Miss Spigot and Miss Pilchard. "Who'd a thought it?"

"And why ever shouldn't they?" demanded Miss Pilchard.

"Why indeed?" asked Miss Spigot archly. "You made it, Amelia dear, so you should know! Cocoa everyone? Bananas? I do think it's important that we keep up our strength!"

"That's only what's right," agreed Mrs Muldoon. "If we was to collapse then where would they be? It's got to be faced. It's us that's in charge."

"And us to pay," added Miss Spigot. "Should anything go wrong."

"So I've told them out there," continued Mrs Muldoon, nodding in the direction of the dining room. "Clean plates and no monkey tricks! We are well and truly snowed up and the snow ploughs could be Some Time and should we lose anyone through starvation or carelessness then it's us will look bad . . ."

"But should we keep them . . ." interrupted Miss Pilchard eagerly.

"Through thick and thin," said Miss Spigot.

"Fair means or foul!"

"Against all odds!"

"Then," said Mrs Muldoon, "We will be National Heroines and Dames sure as fate and a pension to boot I shouldn't wonder."

"Oh," murmured Amelia Pilchard, swaying with closed eyes and clasped hands, "I see cheering crowds! . . . What can it mean? And it seems to be raining . . ."

Miss Spigot and Mrs Muldoon glanced at each other in alarm.

". . . Roses and lilies!"

"She's got a lovely gift!" whispered Mrs Muldoon, enraptured, and Miss Spigot nodded in agreement.

In the dining room the lights were flickering

and flickering, causing Charlotte and Emma to shiver with misery. Without them the school would be totally dark, the windows by now being completely blotted out with snow.

"It must be because Mr Bedwig's solar panels are getting snowed up," said Madeline suddenly. "You know, he fixed them up last term to run the lights and heat the boiler. That can't be working properly either. No wonder it's got so cold."

"We'll die then," sobbed Charlotte. "We'll freeze in the dark!"

"Of course we won't," said Madeline. "Someone will have to go up and dig them out, that's all. I don't mind doing it."

"I'll come with you," offered Dougal. "I've got wellies."

"Mrs Muldoon said no monkey tricks," Samantha reminded them. "Don't you think getting up on the roof . . ."

"Mrs Muldoon needn't know," interrupted Dougal robustly. "It'll only take a minute to tunnel up through the snow in the playground. Quick scrape, pop back down . . ."

Simon, who had disappeared a few minutes earlier, returned at that moment looking quite white.

"Come and see," he said urgently. "I've just looked outside. I opened the cloakroom door . . ."

Outside the door that lead into the playground was a solid wall of snow. It creaked. It was as stiff as deep frozen ice cream. It dented when kicked but did not crumble.

"You can't tunnel through that," said Simon Percy.

There was a short, gloomy silence during which all the lights went out. It was broken by Madeline who exclaimed triumphantly.

"Look, there's a skylight! Just over our heads! That grey square, in the ceiling. We've only to get through that and we'll be right beside the solar panels! We just need to get some ladders!"

Getting the ladders (which were stored in the basement) in the pitch dark, without attracting the attention of the dinner ladies, was not exactly easy. The trapdoor that led to the basement from under the teacher's desk in Class 4b was a great help, however, and so was the extreme tidiness of the basement, untouched since the days of Mr Bedwig. Once the ladders had been located, a human chain was formed from trapdoor to cloakroom and they were passed from hand to hand in the darkness.

"Now then!" whispered Kate, when the ladders were finally in place, propped against a row of coatpegs with herself to hold them steady. "Wellies on, Dougal darling! And coat and scarf! And you too, Madeline! Simon and Samuel, guard the door, and if you hear the dinner ladies coming, rush and distract them! Up you go then, Dougal!"

"I've brought Mr Bedwig's broom to help us sweep," Madeline said. "Can you take it, Kate, and pass it up? Oh!"

An avalanche of snow fell into the cloakroom as Dougal, high above their heads in the darkness, pushed open the skylight. A square of grey sky appeared, blotted out almost straight away by a second avalanche as Dougal heaved himself out.

"What's it like?" called Kate, but Dougal for once in his life, was lost for words, and Madeline, climbing out beside him, could only gasp.

Fourteen metres of snow made an amazing difference to the landscape. Pudding Bag School now appeared as nothing more than two short, stumpy triangles of roof. Pudding Bag Lane had entirely disappeared. The church tower on its opposite side was marked by a huge, curving snowdrift. All fences, boundaries, street lights and telephone lines were gone. All trees were gone, except the most enormous, which were a tangle of the topmost twigs, poking out through the white. To the south there was nothing to be seen but banks of swirling fog, but to the north the multi-storey office blocks of London rose grey and ghostly in the mist, half their usual height. The humming that Madeline had noticed earlier that morning was now explained. Dozens and dozens of helicopters were disappearing into the north.

"What's it *like*?" called Kate plaintively, from under their feet.

"Fantastic!" shouted Dougal.

"Has it stopped snowing?"

"Oh yes!"

"Can you walk on it safely?"

"Yes, yes, it's frozen solid!"

"Get on with it then, Dougal darling," said Kate. "It's awfully dark down here. Is Madeline all right?"

"Quite all right," called Madeline, pulling herself together and making her way to the nearest solar panel. They were easy to find, a double line of them along the line of the rooftop, drifted up in sweeping curves, but still above the level of the snow. She began to sweep and Dougal, following her, scooped and scraped with his hands and before long a faint cheer from below told them that the lights were back on.

"Come down now!" called Kate. "Simon says the dinner ladies are beginning to lay the tables for lunch. They'll be looking for us in a minute."

They climbed down reluctantly and were assailed by an amazing smell of fish.

"Lunch," said Kate. "Brace yourselves!"

Lunch however, was surprisingly edible and the dinner ladies cheered both by Amelia Pilchard's glowing visions and the miraculous return of electricity, sang as they served.

Lavender's blue, diddle diddle,
Lavender's green.
When you are king, diddle diddle . . .
I shall be . . .

Here they broke off giggling, because Queen was too much to hope for, even Amelia couldn't quite imagine that. Presently, however, they found new words.

Lavender's blue, diddle diddle
Vi'lets the same.
When we escape, diddle diddle,
I'll be a . . .

Class 4b could not quite make out the last word, it was lost in gales of laughter. Nor could they decide exactly what was in the fish cakes.

"Tapioca of course," said Kate, who had already realised that tapioca went into nearly everything the dinner ladies cooked. "But there's something else that makes them that lovely pink."

Whatever it was, it was greatly enjoyed and second helpings were accepted very cheerfully. Only Madeline and Bagdemagus seemed not to be happy. Madeline was preoccupied with the memory of the dozens of helicopters she had seen disappearing over the horizon and did not notice what she ate. Nobody knew what was the matter with Bagdemagus. He prowled round the table, spitting and swearing and arching in fury whenever a dinner lady passed.

Pudding was plain tapioca but everyone was too full up to mind.

After lunch the dinner ladies withdrew to the kitchen to celebrate their success with Horlicks and oven chips and afternoon naps. As soon as they were safely out of the way Class 4b divided into two groups. The more intrepid (led by Dougal McDougal) spent an exciting afternoon tobogganing on the school roof. The others began a careful search for somewhere to sleep that night.

"Because we must find somewhere better than that classroom floor," said Kate. "Just in case we are not rescued today."

It was Madeline who thought of the basement, and as soon as she suggested it everyone realised that it was the perfect place. It was warm, heated by the solar-powered boiler, and draught free, and had no blank, snow blotted windows to show the white-faced reflections that had been so unnerving the night before. Also it had a wholesome feel about it, a sort of echo of Mr Bedwig himself, reassuring and cheerful and matter of fact.

"It's just like he's only this minute gone away," said Samantha.

"I wonder if he's worrying about us."

"Mummy will be worrying," remarked Charlotte dolefully, "and Daddy! Daddy will be frantic, won't he, Emma?"

"Think how pleased they'll be when they discover you're perfectly safe," said Kate hastily, seeing the twins were once more on the brink of tears. "What's that you've found Madeline?"

It was a small transistor radio, and very shortly they discovered that no one was worrying about them at all.

". . . The successful evacuation of blizzard-bound London," came a smug newsreader's voice between bursts of static. ". . . Entire population helicopter-lifted . . . sun-soaked north!"

"That's what those helicopters were doing!" exclaimed Madeline.

". . . Triumph of planning . . . not a single casualty, complaint or missing person report has been received!"

"What about us?" squeaked Samantha indignantly.

". . . Temporary schools . . ."

"Listen! Listen!" said Kate.

". . . in empty Scottish castles . . . hospitals all moved to the invigorating air of low season holiday camps . . ."

The voice was getting fainter and fainter, as if the speaker was drifting further and further away.

". . . Government ministers congratulated . . . no cause for alarm . . . contact numbers for families to be announced in the next few days . . ."

The sound was growing fainter and fainter.

"The batteries must be nearly flat," said Madeline.

". . . much needed boost for Scottish economy . . . Weather forecast . . ."

But to everyone's great disappointment the sound faded completely before the weather forecast could begin.

"Blinkin' 'eck!" said Mrs Muldoon, peering out through a crack of open kitchen door when Kate went to tell her the news. "Everyone's gone, did you say?"

"I'm afraid so."

"Parked the schools in empty castles, have they?"

"That's what we heard."

"Not noticed they haven't got us then?"

"They don't seem to have."

"Won't be coming to rescue us then while this weather lasts."

"Don't you think so?"

"Stands to reason! Pity you didn't get the

forecast! Thunder by the sound!"

"Wrong, Lacie dear!"

Amelia Pilchard had materialised suddenly in the corridor behind Kate.

"Wrong, wrong, wrong! Lacie dear," she repeated. "That's not thunder. That's Something On The Roof and Pansy and I know what!"

"Kiddies!" said Miss Spigot, popping up behind her. "That brother of Young Kate's here, and his gang! Up there with tea trays! I ask you!"

"Never!" exclaimed Mrs Muldoon.

"Got a ladder in the cloakroom," continued Miss Spigot. "The young rips! Amelia slipped up a moment ago and caught them red handed!"

"Oh, I'm sure they didn't mean any harm!" exclaimed Kate, but it was no use. That was the end of the tobogganing on the roof. Mrs Muldoon, already upset by the radio news, was very angry indeed. She did not wish, she said, to be held responsible for young persons hurling themselves to their deaths, and Miss Spigot and Miss

Pilchard completely agreed.

Class 4b were told that they were in disgrace. There was no repeat of the lunch-time concert of "Lavender's Blue" that evening. At suppertime plates of bubble and squeak and rabbit stew were handed round with such grim expressions that nobody liked to even attempt analysing their contents until the dinner ladies were safely back in the kitchen.

"They do like to keep that kitchen door tight shut," remarked Samuel Moon.

"They think that way they'll keep us from knowing what we're eating," said Dougal. "They won't though! Right then! Potato and that cabbage again, that's the bubble and squeak. Can anyone work out what's in this stew?"

"Beetroot, tapioca," said Madeline, sorting carefully with her fork, "and the brown stuff must be rabbit I suppose. I didn't know rabbit was so nasty. I've never had it before."

Bagdemagus supervised the consumption of rabbit stew with unconcealed fury.

Bagdemagus knows something, wrote Simon Percy in his diary after supper that night. *I wonder what*.

CHAPTER THREE

What Bagdemagus Knew

By night time the camp in the basement was complete. Amelia Pilchard (prowling the empty classrooms for her own private purposes) had inspected it and said it gave her the cold horrors. Mrs Muldoon and Miss Spigot (walking off their late supper of chicken nuggets and poptarts) said it put them in mind of an open grave, but Class 4b loved it. It was wonderfully homely. Sledging clothes steamed cosily on the hot water pipes and boots and shoes dried on the boiler. The games cupboard had been emptied and the sleeping arrangements (constructed on two levels so as to save floor space) were now in place. Excellent multiperson hammocks had been made by hanging football and cricket nets from the floor joists of the classrooms above. Beneath them several thicknesses of P.E. mats set out in a row made a long, continual mattress. There were no arguments about who should sleep where. At bedtime the more reckless people (led by Dougal McDougal) grabbed the hammocks, while the more prudent (led by Madeline Brown) chose the mattress underneath. When everybody was installed for the night Kate covered them up with the two ancient red velvet curtains that had once adorned Pudding Bag School stage. Then Bagdemagus curled up on Madeline's chest and Kate tucked herself up at the end of the mattress bed and Samuel Moon surprised them all by sitting up and reading aloud from an ancient book of Antarctic exploration that he had discovered in the school library. It told of dripping snow caves and frozen sleeping bags, feasts of raw penguin and seal liver stew, weeks of darkness when the sun never rose above the horizon, journeys so bitter that the sledge runners froze to the ground, ice-covered seas and howling blizzards. Listening as

Samuel's solemn, husky voice described such awfulnesses was very comforting. Even Charlotte and Emma began to think that things might be very much worse. The boiler purred like a cat and the red velvet curtains felt very cosy. One by one Class 4b snuggled down and fell asleep.

Bagdemagus did not purr. He spent a restless night and woke Madeline very early by trampling on her stomach. He waited impatiently as she crawled out of bed, and as

soon as she was properly up seized her firmly by the toe of a sock and tried to drag her up out of the basement.

"Hi! Stop it! Wait till I get my shoes on!" said Madeline.

Bagdemagus sat down and swore while Madeline tied her laces and then led her at a great rate out of the basement, along grey, empty corridors, and eventually to the kitchen door.

"Do you want me to knock for you?" asked Madeline, very puzzled.

Bagdemagus shook his head emphatically.

"What then?"

Madeline, Bagdemagus indicated rather impatiently, should observe the large and smelly dustbin which had been parked outside the kitchen door by the dinner ladies the night before.

"Oh, that!" said Madeline, and was about to lift the lid when Mrs Muldoon appeared, bustling suddenly from the kitchen with a pile of plates and a seething saucepan.

"Now then young lady," said Mrs Muldoon. "No call for you to be a-poking and a-prying round here!"

"I wasn't," said Madeline. "Only Bagdemagus seemed to want to show me this dustbin. Is it here for anything special?"

"It is where it is," said Mrs Muldoon with dignity, "Because my assistants and I did not wish to sleep with it. Miss Nosey Parker! Spoons, Amelia dear!"

"Coming!" called Miss Pilchard, and a moment later came in carrying a bunch of spoons, each of which she polished with a fog of breath and a rub with a small furry rag before arranging them daintily around the table.

"No children here but this one?" she enquired between huffs.

"None but her," agreed Mrs Muldoon. "Pansy still busy?"

"Topping and tailing," said Miss Pilchard. "Fiddly, she says."

"This one's been enquiring about the bin," Mrs Muldoon informed her, and she winked heavily as she nodded towards Madeline.

Amelia Pilchard darted a very cold look at Madeline as she laid down the last of the spoons. She had opened her mouth as if to speak when both dinner ladies were distracted by the arrival of the rest of Class 4b, clattering into the dining hall. Nudged to it by Bagdemagus, Madeline opened the lid of the dustbin and peered swiftly inside.

"Cat food tins," she told her classmates later on when breakfast (tapioca and potato porridge) had been consumed and they were crowded together in one of the cloakrooms, washing faces and tidying hair and cleaning teeth with fingers dipped in dining room salt (Kate's idea).

"Perhaps he was trying to tell you he was hungry," suggested Simon.

"Perhaps," agreed Madeline uncertainly. "But if he's eaten all those tins I don't see how . . . Oh, no! Oh Simon! I've just remembered! The classroom pets! All this time we've been snowed up here and nobody has even thought about the classroom pets!"

Bagdemagus and his problems were temporarily abandoned as Class 4b, worried and repentant, hurried to the rescue. The Infant's gerbil colony had been forgotten for nearly two days. So had Class 4a's stick insects, the office goldfish, the guinea pig family, Ant Planet (an over-populated perspex and plastic dome donated by an ant-phobic parent), and the pedigree black-and-white mice.

"There aren't half as many as there used to be," remarked Simon Percy, as he filled up the gerbils' feeding bowls. "When I was an Infant there seemed to be thousands! Same with the stick insects."

"There still are an awful lot of stick insects," remarked Samantha with a shudder. "Don't look at me like that Madeline! I don't mind being brave about being snowed up and eating the dinner ladies' cooking and sleeping in the basement and nobody knowing we are here, but I *can't* be brave about stick insects!"

"Neither can I really," agreed Madeline. "I pretend I don't mind them, but I do. I was wondering if we ought to take all the pets down to the basement with us, but I couldn't bear the stick insects. They have such eyes! And the goldfish tank and the gerbils are too heavy to lift and just looking at Ant Planet makes me itch all over. So I suppose we might as well leave things where they are. Except for Bagdemagus of course."

Madeline looked worriedly at Bagdemagus as she spoke. He was still in a terrible temper.

"He has gone thin!" exclaimed Simon suddenly.

"Bagdemagus has?"

"Yes, look at him! He looks like he's going down, like a really old balloon. He used to look so bouncy and he doesn't anymore." Madeline bent down and burrowed her fingers into Bagdemagus's thick, marmalade coat and found that Simon was quite right. Underneath his fur Bagdemagus was quite bony. She thought of the empty cat food tins and she thought of Bagdemagus, growling with temper around the dustbin and she was struck by a horrible idea. And then she pushed the idea to the back of her mind and hurried off to the kitchen where the cat food was kept to beg an early lunch for Bagdemagus.

Amelia Pilchard opened the door and

on hearing Madeline's request very begrudgingly produced a half-filled tin of Whiskas, which Bagdemagus devoured in three starving gulps.

"I think he'd like some more," said Madeline.

"There is no more," said Miss Pilchard briefly, and Madeline pushed her horrible idea even further to the back of her mind. Instead she enquired about the strange, earthy, fusty, smell that was escaping from the kitchen.

"Nut roast," Amelia Pilchard told her. "Now off with you both!"

Madeline, returning through the entrance hall, was not very surprised to notice that the collages entitled "Our Autumn Harvest" that had decorated its walls for weeks, had mysteriously disappeared.

The nut roast was accompanied by Crispy Pancake Rolls and Dougal McDougal found something very strange in his.

"It's a hairclip," he said, spitting it out and inspecting it.

"It's not," said Kate, peering over to look.

"One of those things for scraping out your nails then!"

"Don't be revolting, Dougal Darling! Anyway, it's not one of those."

"Or for putting on mascara!"

"Of course it isn't! What's it made of?"

"Plastic I think."

"It must be one of those little toys they give away in cereal packets and it's got mixed up with the cooking somehow," said Kate. "Or a broken bit of one. I've seen something like it before. Throw it away Dougal Darling! Thank goodness you didn't choke!"

Dougal put it in his pocket and forgot about it.

"Forty-eight hours, Dames Pansy and Pilchard!" said Mrs Muldoon. "Forty-eight hours and not a soul have we lost or a meal have they missed! Pansy dear, are you starting supper already? What did you decide should be done with the you-know-what's that were so fiddly to top and tail?"

"Kebabs," replied Miss Spigot, squinting

sideways at her handiwork as she rammed home the skewers. "I'm kebabing them! It is a well-known fact, Dame Lacie, that kiddies will eat anything that is stuck on a stick. And Amelia is doing a nice tapioca Shape coloured with the last of the beetroot for afters. Should you say three life-long pensions for services to humanity were in the bag, Lacie dear?"

Mrs Muldoon said that if there was any justice in the world the money was as good theirs to spend already, and Amelia Pilchard closed her eyes and in a visionary trance saw them all in a National Tribute on prime time TV. She described it so well that very soon Mrs Muldoon and Miss Spigot saw it too. It was all very gratifying (though no more than they deserved) and they were all three of them in a very good temper when Kate knocked on the door. Kate asked if it would be all right if she went up on to the roof to see if there were any signs of help arriving.

"After all," remarked Mrs Muldoon, when Kate had been given their gracious approval and gone off to fetch the ladder. "Somebody's got to, I suppose, and if push comes to shove it's not as if she is one of ours!" Which meant, as the other two dinner ladies completely understood, that if Kate fell to her death or was lost in the snow or anything else of that kind then they could not possibly be held responsible.

Kate, standing on the ladder with her head and shoulders out of the skylight, was astonished to see sunshine and blue sky. No snow had fallen since the night before, the tracks of the roof tobogganing party were as clear and sharp as if they had just been made. She reached out to touch a blue-shadowed footprint and found that the snow was as hard as ice. There was no sign of life in any direction, not a sound, or a movement, or a bird in the sky. Nor was there anything, Kate realised, that would show any passing helicopter that a class full of children and three dinner ladies were stranded deep in the snow beneath.

We should make a sign, thought Kate. A cross that someone could see flying over.

"I need something black," she called

down the ladder to Class 4b, waiting below. "Something black that will show up on the snow and make a mark for the rescue helicopters to see."

"*Are* there rescue helicopters?" asked Charlotte hopefully.

"Bound to be dozens," said Kate as cheerfully as she could, considering the emptiness of the sky. "Now what can we use? Soot would do."

"What about black powder paint?" asked Emma and was very pleased when Kate said at once that powder paint would be perfect.

Several people ran off to hunt for some straight away and half-a-dozen tins were collected from various art cupboards and handed up the ladder. Soon Kate was out on the roof, marking a large but rather wobbly cross over the lumps and bumps of the surrounding snowdrifts.

"There!" she said, coming down frozen and black but triumphant. "Anyone could see that for miles! And if it snows more I will just go out and do it again."

"Until someone comes?" asked Charlotte.

"That's right," said Kate hopefully. "Until someone comes."

The tapioca Shape coloured with the last of the beetroot was most unpleasant, but the kebabs were utterly delicious. Only Madeline did not enjoy them. She gave hers to Bagdemagus who took it with a very knowing kind of look.

"What's the matter, Madeline?" asked Charlotte from across the table.

"Nothing," said Madeline untruthfully, and was very glad that Bagdemagus could not talk.

Dougal McDougal was the next one to understand. He fell out of his hammock in the middle of the night, landing on top of Madeline, and bring Simon Percy down with him.

"I dreamed about my pancake roll," he began announcing, even before he had picked himself up. "I dreamed about my pancake roll and I . . ."

"Shush! Shush!" whispered Madeline.

"You'll wake everyone up!"

". . . dreamed about that thing I found in it . . ." he began fishing about in his pocket, ". . . and I suddenly knew . . ."

"Stop talking so loudly!" said Madeline. "Come up to the classroom. Simon, come on! Get his other arm! Make him come out of the basement before he gets everyone up!"

"Why?" asked Simon, still groggy with sleep. "What's all the fuss about? What's the matter with Dougal? What's going on?"

"No wonder they were crispy! Oh, all right Madeline, I'm coming!"

"*What* were crispy?" asked Simon plaintively, as he followed Dougal and Madeline up the step ladder that led into their classroom. "Why are we coming up here in the middle of the night?"

"A stick insect's leg!" said Dougal. "That's what it was! A stick insect's leg! No wonder Kate thought she'd seen one before! And I don't see why we're being so careful to be quiet, Madeline Brown!"

Madeline carefully closed the trapdoor and sat on it before replying.

"Imagine the twins if they knew they'd eaten Crispy Stick Insect Pancake Rolls!"

"Crispy Stick Insect Pancake Rolls!" repeated Simon Percy in horror.

"Yes, or cat food fishcakes!"

"Cat food fishcakes!"

"Prime Cut Salmon Whiskas we ate, and Rabbit Chunks with Savoury Jelly!"

Simon and Dougal stared at her, speechless and green.

"It's true! I saw the tins in the dustbin. Bagdemagus showed me. He knew."

"When did *you* know?" demanded Dougal accusingly.

"I only really *believed* at suppertime. When I saw those kebabs . . ."

"What!"

"And remembered what Simon said about the gerbils. How there used to be thousands . . ."

"I'm going to wake everyone up and tell them right now!" said Dougal.

"You mustn't," said Madeline. "It would just make them sick, and what's the point of that? And people like Charlotte and Emma will be really frightened. And after all, I suppose it's better than actually starving . . ."

Simon and Dougal looked at her in amazement.

"Actually starving," repeated Dougal slowly, and he looked round at the bleak, snow-buried windows, and the empty classroom.

The date on the blackboard was now three

days old. The tulips on Miss Gilhoolie's desk had dropped their petals and died. It all seemed suddenly to be very bleak and lonely, but just then Bagdemagus appeared from the shadows, climbed onto Dougal's lap, and began to purr.

After all Bagdemagus eats cat food, wrote Simon in his diary the next morning. *And he's all right*.

CHAPTER FOUR

Something Else to Cook

"We must find the dinner ladies something else to cook," said Madeline the next morning. After a breakfast of fried beetroot and tapioca Shape, that did not seem unreasonable to anyone. So the great food hunt began.

Simon Percy recorded the results in his diary.

From the Cloakrooms
7 half packets of crisps (rubbish bins)
4 very old apples (one bitten)
1 banana and 1/2 packet of Rolos (under radiator)
1 packet of baby rusks (some missing) from Infant's shoe bag

From Class 4a's Kitchen Art Exibition

2 carrots, 2 onions, 1 leek and 1/2 a pickled cabbage

From the lockers
27 packets of sweets with one left in the bottom
1 baby rusk
1 Cornish pasty (given to Bagdemagus)

From the teachers' desks
122 packets of confiscated chewing gum
1 box of Mr Kipling Fondant Fancies (2 missing)

Also
1 packet mustard and cress seed
14 bean bags (PE cupboard)

The sweets were shared out and eaten immediately. Charlotte and Emma were handed the mustard and cress to plant, which they did with a mixture of awful pride (at being given such an important responsibility) and awful fear (at the thought of still being snowed up when it was ready to harvest). The baby rusks were put aside for a dire emergency ("Direr than this," said Kate), but the whole of the rest was handed over to the dinner ladies, who received it with great relief. They had their own private list of food supplies pinned up on the kitchen wall, and it was worryingly short (and alive). It was:

Tapioca (very little left)
14 gerbils
3 fish
4 guinea pigs
11 black and white mice
and Bagdemagus

"And when that is gone," said Mrs Muldoon, "we will be down to Rock Bottom and you know what that means!"

Miss Pilchard and Miss Spigot knew very well what it meant. Rock Bottom was the supply of odds and ends of school dinner food in the Emergency Freezer that they were keeping for their own private consumption.

"Not that it is anything like the Good Home Cooking the kiddies are getting," Miss Spigot often remarked as she rooted round for Dino Burgers or Instant Trifle or whatever was on the menu for the dinner ladies that day.

Over the next three days the results of the

great food hunt were recycled into:

Mixed Fruit Pudding
Bean and Vegetable Curry
Bean Hot Pot
Vegetable Bake with Crispy Topping
Bean Surprise (twice)

During this time more snow fell so that the solar panels had to be cleared again and again. It was always Kate who went up on to the roof to do this job, and each time she found it more and more difficult and depressing. There was never any sign of rescue on the way. She would have given up bothering to mark the powder paint cross on the snow altogether if the twins had not constantly reminded her. Charlotte and Emma had cheered up remarkably over the last few days, especially since their mustard and cress had begun to sprout.

Simon Percy kept a careful account of the meals produced by the dinner ladies on the days following the food hunt, and ticked them off against the list of supplies in his diary as they went along. Therefore it was a great shock to him when, on the evening of the third day, supper was not Mr Kipling Fondant Fancies and Chewing Gum (as he had confidently expected), but Golden Tapioca Fish Fingers instead.

It was such a relief to eat food that did not taste of ancient and fusty PE cupboard bean bags that most of Class 4b ate their fish fingers without a second thought. Dougal did pause to whisper, "Cat food, probably!" to Madeline, before tucking in with gusto, but Madeline could not agree. She offered her fish finger to Bagdemagus, who ate it with melancholy, downcast eyes. Madeline caught Simon's glance as he watched and gave a tiny nod of understanding.

"The office goldfish," they told each other, with one wordless look.

That night when they were all in bed Samuel Moon described to them a desperate rescue that he had read about that afternoon.

"They were marooned," he said. "On a little stony island. Their ship had sunk and they had eaten nearly all the food . . ."

"There's still our mustard and cress," said Charlotte. "Growing all the time!"

"And nobody came to rescue them," went on Samuel. "Nobody could because nobody knew they were there . . ."

Madeline gave a little sigh.

"And it was terrible weather of course."

"So what did they do?" interrupted Dougal. "Die?"

"Shut up, Dougal Darling," said Kate briskly. "Of course they didn't die, did they, Samuel?"

"No," said Samuel. "None of them died. They had a few supplies left, just enough for a rescue party to set out with . . ."

"Oh, oh!" began Emma and Charlotte excitedly, both struck with the same brilliant idea at once. "Oh, we've thought of something! Go on, Samuel!"

"So a few of them packed up and left the others. They travelled north. They sailed away in an open boat . . ."

"Oh," said Charlotte and Emma, very disappointed all of a sudden. "We haven't got an open boat."

"But they did find help?" said Madeline.

"Yes."

"And they got back in time to rescue their friends?"

"Yes, yes!"

"Before they had to eat the cat?"

"What!"

"I didn't mean to say that," said Madeline hastily. "I got muddled up. But that's what we are going to have to do, the same as them. And we will travel north like they did, because that's where the radio said everyone had gone to . . ."

"The dinner ladies will never let you," said Samantha.

"We'll go without telling them."

"How will you get out? They keep the ladder in the kitchen and all the doors are blocked with tons and tons of snow."

"We'll dig a tunnel."

"They'll notice."

"They would if we dug it out from one of the doors," said Madeline. "But we won't do that. Don't you remember when Mr Bedwig was here? How he made us an escape passage through the place in the basement where the coal used to come in, so that we could get out of school without Mr Jones knowing?"

"But, Madeline," protested Kate at this point. "Don't you think it might be dangerous?"

"It's the only thing to do," said Madeline, and Class 4b were reminded of the time when Madeline had decided the only thing to do was to blast their terrible headmaster into deepest space. Madeline was usually so small and quiet that it was hard to believe that she had such astonishing ideas, but she had been quite right then, and probably she was quite right now.

"We will need a tent or something like that to sleep in," she said.

"Madeline!" said Kate. "It's not *camping* weather!"

"It is," said Samuel earnestly. "They camped out in the Antarctic in much worse weather than this, Kate. And a tent would be much quicker than having to build an igloo every night."

"Sleeping bags," said Madeline. "Supplies . . ."

"It is very important not to get scurvy," said Samuel. "You will need plenty of vegetables."

"Mustard and cress is vegetables," said Emma.

"Just the thing," said Madeline. "And a sledge to carry it all on!"

"How will you know which way to *go*?" asked Samantha.

"Easy in the daytime," said Madeline. "North is where the tower blocks are thickest. I expect you can still see them sticking up, can't you Kate?"

"Bits of them," said Kate dubiously.

"And there will be stars at night."

"Not if it's snowing," pointed out Kate. "And it's been foggy a lot lately too."

"Well, we'll take Bagdemagus," said Madeline, suddenly inspired. "Cats always know their way home, everyone knows that! We'll take Bagdemagus and which ever way he points we'll go in the opposite direction! As long as we start off going north he will always point South. He can be a compass cat!"

"Who'll go?" asked Samantha, and there was silence.

That afternoon Kate had found a candle in an ancient cardboard box. It was made of beeswax.

"I remember that candle," Simon Percy had remarked when he saw it. "It's from when we did our Bee Project, ages ago, when we were Infants. We went to a farm and saw honey being made."

"On a boiling hot day," said Dougal, joining in. "You couldn't eat the ice cream fast enough to stop it melting."

"It was proper countryside," said Samuel Moon dreamily.

"We had a picnic in a field that was all covered in buttercups," said Madeline. "And when you lay down and looked up it was like they whirred above your head like planets. And Simon said, "Why does the ground hum?" And the farmer said, 'Because it's alive.' "

"I remember," said Simon.

"And we brought back honey fudge and pencils with bees on their tops and a real honeycomb and that candle."

Now the candle was alight, filling the basement with the hot sweet scent of summer. It was very quiet and still. Only Bagdemagus was restless, his prowling shadow moving among shadows on the wall. Shadows of hammocks, shadow boots and shadow books and shadow heads hung in thought.

"I'll go," said Charlotte. "If somebody will come with me."

"I will," said Emma at once. "And there'll be Madeline, won't there Madeline?"

Madeline nodded while the rest of Class 4b stared at the twins with a mixture of astonishment and shame. That candle-lit memory of summer had been too much for most of them. It was one thing to plan a winter journey across a deserted, snow-buried city, but it was quite another to say you would actually go. Even Madeline, who had known from the start that she would not escape, shivered at the thought.

Now she said, "I don't think both twins ought to go."

"I don't think anyone ought to go," said Kate. "Don't look at me like that Dougal darling! And don't say what I think you're going to say!"

"Well I'm getting sick of being stuck indoors," said Dougal. "Anyway it might be quite fun."

"It couldn't be any worse than the Antarctic was," agreed Samuel. "I don't mind going."

"Good," said Dougal. "That should be enough then. Sam. He's the Antarctic expert. Me. I'm not being left out. Madeline because she thought of it, and one of the twins but not both in case we don't make it! No good you sticking your hand up like that, Simon! You get asthma, you know you do! And don't bother saying you'll come, Kate, because they'll need you here. Somebody's got to keep the solar panels clear and make sure the dinner ladies don't cook Samantha. And I'm not a bit tired. I'm going to get up again! I think we ought to start getting ready tonight! Simon might be right, and it might be Fondant

Fancies and chewing gum for breakfast, but if he's wrong, there's no time to waste!"

"Shut up Dougal!" said Madeline and Simon.

"No," said Dougal. "We ought to tell them if they are going to be left behind with the dinner ladies."

It was too late after that to stop, and Class 4b were informed by Dougal (with a certain amount of relish) that they had eaten the cat food, the office goldfish, most of the gerbils and the stick insects already, that the supplies they had discovered on the great food hunt had been almost consumed, and that it was only a matter of time until . . .

Here everyone stopped listening and jumped out of bed and the preparations for the Relief Expedition North began at once.

Icy cold and musty-smelling air filled the basement as Mr Bedwig's escape passage was opened up for the first time for months. To everyone's delight the Christmas lights, which were strung along its winding length, were found to be still working. The passage ended in steps and a double trapdoor that, in normal weather, opened out on to Pudding Bag Lane. Now, of course, it opened out on to snow.

"You'll never get through that," said Kate thankfully. "It's solid ice."

"We will," said Madeline. "We'll have to. Don't you see that we'll have to, Kate?"

"Of course she does," said Dougal.

After the escape passage had been opened up and inspected, people turned to searching through the basement cupboards for anything that might possibly be of any use.

"If only we could find something else for the dinner ladies to cook," said Samantha, who had taken very much to heart Dougal's second reason for Kate not to join the expedition.

"He was joking," Kate told her, as comfortingly as she could, but Samantha was infinitely more comforted by the discovery she made herself a few minutes later. A huge pile of bean bags, bursting at the seams and put aside for repair, but still, as Samantha said joyfully, perfectly edible.

"Well done Samantha!" said Kate, "And

look what I've found! Nearly a whole sack-full too!"

"What is it?" demanded a circle of excited people.

"Grass seed!"

"What's grass seed doing down here?"

"Mr Bedwig put grass seed over the bonfire site where we launched the rocket from," remembered Simon Percy. "It must be left over from that."

"But can you eat grass seed?"

"Oh yes," said Simon at once. "My parents lived on stuff like that when their hot air balloon crashed in the Himalayan foothills. Especially before they tamed the yaks."

"That's all right then," said Samantha, sighing with relief.

"Yes," said Kate. "Now they won't have to go."

But the members of the relief expedition said immediately that this was not so. It was either a case of going now, they explained, leaving everyone behind eating grass seed and beanbags, or going in three or four days time, when the grass seed and beanbags had run out, leaving everyone behind . . .

"Eating Samantha," said Dougal.

"But we might be rescued any day," said Kate.

"If you are," said Madeline, "you can come and look for us. But I don't think we will be. I don't think anyone even knows we are here. I think our families just think we are living in some remote Scottish castle not bothering to write."

Kate stopped arguing after that and told herself that anyway no one could go anywhere until a tunnel had been dug, not to mention a sledge and tent and sleeping bags conjured up from nowhere. She took herself to bed, hoping everyone else would follow her example, but all around her the preparations for the relief expedition went on far into the night.

CHAPTER FIVE

Bean Bags and Grass Seed

Samuel Moon had the sort of watch that could be programmed to ring an alarm.

"Thank goodness!" said Class 4b, who had decided that the sooner the grass seed and bean bags were delivered to the dinner ladies the next morning, the better it would be. Breakfast might, as some people still tried to hope, be Fondant Fancies and chewing gum, but on the other hand it might not. Class 4b thought of the guinea pigs and gerbils and black-and-white mice and (so that breakfast should cause no unnecessary bloodshed), set Samuel's alarm for five o'clock in the morning.

Five minutes after it went off he and Dougal and Simon Percy had arrived at the kitchen door.

"I expect they're still asleep in there," said Dougal. "Better bash really hard if we want to wake them up! Stand back and I'll . . . Oh!"

Even before he had raised his hand, the kitchen door began to open. For a moment, seeing the grey emptiness that lay behind, they thought it had done it of its own accord, but then into the nothingness Miss Pilchard appeared. She wore a large plastic apron and pink rubber gloves, and clasped a very big pair of kitchen scissors.

"What a delicious surprise!" she remarked, showing no surprise at all, and she snipped absentmindedly with her scissors at the air in front of her. The blades made a lively, scrunching sound as they opened and shut.

"Crikey, Miss Pilchard!" exclaimed Dougal McDougal, considerably startled at this unexpected appearance. "Crikey, Miss Pilchard! You do look . . . er . . . you do look . . ."

Dougal's voice trailed into silence. Miss Pilchard was looking down at the three of them with a sort of cold, thinking curiosity, as if planning how she would eke them out,

81

should it ever come to cooking in the end. It was such a look that Samuel could not stand it. He dumped his burden of bean bags and fled back to the basement.

Simon would have liked very much to follow Samuel, but Miss Pilchard's gaze was now concentrated upon Dougal and himself. Dougal seemed to be still completely mesmerised and was no help at all, so it was Simon who ended up explaining, in a surprised sort of squeak:

"We found this stuff in one of the basement cupboards, Miss Pilchard. We thought it would do for cooking."

Snack! went the scissors blades, one last time.

"More or less anything will do for cooking," remarked Miss Pilchard, and she smiled tenderly at the place where Samuel had stood.

"There's loads of bean bags," Simon told her, with a sort of desperate eagerness. "And all this grass seed which we thought . . . Oh, Mrs Muldoon!"

Mrs Muldoon, shoeless and rumpled and puffy with sleep, had never looked so beautiful as she did to Simon and Dougal at that moment. Everything suddenly became normal again. Dougal came out of his trance, and Simon, speaking in quite a different voice, explained, "We were just showing Miss Pilchard the things we found last night!"

"Food!" said Dougal.

"Grass seed," said Miss Pilchard, looking at Dougal with dislike. "Grass seed, Mrs Muldoon, and more of those beans. It seems we will have to devise a vegetarian menu after all!"

Dougal and Simon glanced at each other and longed to speak.

"Grass seed and beans are all very well," said Mrs Muldoon. "Not what one would wish perhaps, but I daresay you will make an art form of the ekeing, Miss Pilchard, as you always do!"

Dougal gave a sudden snort of laughter, which he tried unsuccessfully to turn into a cough.

"But if you were to ask me, Miss Pilchard," continued Mrs Muldoon, glaring at Dougal. "I would say grass seed and beans was not the half of it! Guilty as guilty, these two look! What have you been up to, out of bed so early? Messing about on that roof?"

"No, no!" Dougal and Simon assured her at once.

"I won't have you poking through the dustbins. I told that Madeline so the other day!"

"We haven't been doing! We haven't done anything like that!"

"No quarrelling or aguefying or breaking your necks with silly games?"

"No, Mrs Muldoon!"

"I am pleased to hear it," said Mrs Muldoon heavily. "I shouldn't *like* to ask Miss Spigot to spend her nights it that basement with you! I shouldn't *like* to, and I couldn't stick it myself, having a nervous fear of being buried alive. And neither could Miss Pilchard, so highly strung as she is. But only last night Miss Spigot said to me, 'I can and I will, Mrs Muldoon, for the sake of the kiddies! If you ask me to I will!' "

Dougal and Simon looked at each other in unconcealed horror.

"So I give you fair warning," said Mrs Muldoon triumphantly. "Any monkey business and down she will be and there she will stay until rescue arrives. "No sacrifice is too great," she said to me last night. "No sacrifice is too great, Mrs Muldoon, for the sake of those blessed kiddies!" She is a woman in a million and Miss Pilchard here is another, if you did but know it . . ."

Miss Pilchard bowed her head and closed her eyes as if overcome, and Mrs Muldoon turned aside to mop away invisible tears. Dougal and Simon, seeing they were occupied, prudently seized the moment and bolted.

"That's give them something to think about!" commented Mrs Muldoon briskly as she put her handkerchief away, and then seeing that Miss Pilchard's eyes were still shut, asked, "What do you see now, Amelia?"

"Fountains, fountains," replied Miss Pilchard, swaying ever so slightly. "And statues in white marble! What can it mean?"

"It's a beautiful omen, Amelia dear," said Mrs Muldoon.

Meanwhile Samuel Moon had returned to the basement in a state of panic.

"We were only just in time!" he told Class 4b. "She had her rubber gloves on and everything, that horrible Miss Pilchard! She . . ."

"Tell us about it later, Samuel" suggested Kate sleepily. "Right now I think everyone should snuggle down for at least another three hours!"

"She had rubber gloves and a plastic apron and great snapping scissors," said Samuel. "I bet it would have been guinea pig for breakfast if we hadn't arrived when we did! I think everybody should get out of bed at once, and dig for their lives!"

"Dig what?" demanded Kate, yawning and yawning.

"The escape tunnel so that the relief expedition can go for help straight away. She's dead weird, that Miss Pilchard, you ask Dougal and Simon!"

Kate groaned with despair but Samuel's alarm was very infectious and when Simon and Dougal returned a few minutes later they agreed that he was quite right. Work began almost at once, organised by Madeline Brown, who had stayed awake to invent a method of ice tunnel digging while everyone else slept in the middle of the night.

A team of volunteers hacked away at the ice face with whatever came to hand, hammers and screw drivers from the school tool box, cricket bats, unused rocket parts and the long handled shovel that had been used to stoke the boiler in the days before solar power took over. The excavated snow and ice was piled into waste paper bins and the waste paper bins were emptied into the basement sink.

"Then all we have to do," said Madeline, explaining the system as she chipped at the ice with a chisel and mallet. "Is run the hot tap and the ice will disappear like magic! That's the best job. We had better take turns so that everyone gets a chance to warm their hands up!"

Mr Bedwig's escape passage had been the old entrance by which coal was delivered to Pudding Bag School. A wooden trapdoor in

the middle of Pudding Bag Lane had led down a long chute to the boiler room. Mr Bedwig had cleaned it out, painted it white and added Christmas tree lights and steps. Madeline's excavation system worked so efficiently that by eight o'clock that morning the worst of the work was already done. The tunnel through the snow was as long again as the escape passage, sloping steeply upwards and carved along one edge in the form of rough steps.

"I wish I could think of something that we could use for a tent," Madeline said to Simon as they returned together from the ice face for a handwarming session at the basement sink. "I think we are going to have to take one. I read in Samuel's book that an expert eskimo with the right kind of snow could construct an igloo in fifteen to twenty-five minutes, but how do we know we are going to find the right kind of snow?"

"Or an expert eskimo," said Dougal, who was also warming his hands.

Madeline laughed but then looked serious again as she stirred the lumps of excavated ice melting in the sink.

"It needs to be the sort you can cut into blocks, but Kate says the snow on the roof is as soft as soft, too powdery even for snowballs, and this stuff underneath is solid ice."

"You'll think of something," said Simon comfortingly. "You always do! I wonder how the dinner ladies are getting on with the bean bags and grass seed. I'm starving to death!"

Madeline volunteered to go up and see, and also to feed and count the classroom pets. She returned a few minutes later to say that breakfast was ready and that the gerbils and guinea pigs were all present and correct.

"What about the black and white mice?" asked several people. Madeline said nothing, but looked reproachfully across at Bagdemagus who had followed her down the slide. Bagdemagus looked away quickly.

"He's as bad as a dinner lady!" said Samantha, very shocked, but Simon said no, it was not his fault, his cat food was all gone and he had to keep alive.

"Poor Bagdemagus," said Charlotte. "Don't worry, though! There'll be mustard and cress very soon!"

Bagdemagus shrugged his shoulders but looked slightly comforted. Kate bent down and scooped him up.

"He'll just have to learn to eat grass seeds and bean bags like the rest of us," she said cheerfully. "Come on!"

The grass seeds and bean bags had cooked down (with tapioca of course) into a dark grey lumpy porridge that smelt of old shoes. It was served by Miss Spigot, and even she, hardened dinner lady as she was, was forced to avert her eyes as it plopped into the plates. Class 4b, after three hours hard labour in sub-zero temperatures, consumed it with relish. The grass seeds gave the beans and tapioca a bitter, tangy flavour that people found quite delicious.

"And they are the kiddies that complained about the wrong sort of yoghurt and couldn't be got to eat quiche for love nor money!" marvelled Miss Spigot to Mrs Muldoon and Miss Pilchard over their own late breakfast of pot noodles and cocoa. "Even that cat choked a spoonful down!"

"That cat would casserole beautiful with a few of those beans," remarked Miss Pilchard. "Haricot Chat au Fine Herbes, with a pinch of grass seed. They'd never know!"

Simon discovered a perfectly good ground sheet that morning, and Madeline invented a flat-pack igloo that did not need any particular kind of snow.

"Or an expert eskimo!" she said to Dougal McDougal when she erected the display model in the basement for everyone to admire.

Madeline's igloo was made of cardboard boxes. Pudding Bag School had a huge supply of them, stacked up in a corner of the office, waiting to be taken away for recycling. They were the ones that school exercise books were delivered in, and exactly the right size for igloo building.

"But won't they blow away?" asked Kate.

"No, because we will fill them with snow," said Madeline. "And in the mornings all we will have to do is empty them out and fold them flat again and they will be all ready for the next night."

"It's a fantastic idea!" said Dougal. "Isn't it, Kate?"

Kate said that she supposed it was, and resigning herself to the fact that the expedition was really going to happen, set about making four sleeping bags. She used black bin bags and lined them with a double layer of red velvet, chopped from the ends of the stage curtains that they slept under at night. When they were finished they were tested on people brought straight from the furthest end of the ice tunnel. Kate was slightly comforted to see that these people turned from pale blue to bright red in a matter of minutes.

"We will cook in them!" grumbled Dougal to Samuel, but he did not say anything to Kate. His sister was not at all her usual cheerful self that morning. It was snowing heavily again and she had been up on the roof three times already scraping clear the solar panels. Kate hated sewing at the best of times, but sewing with frost bitten fingers, racked with worry, and after a breakfast of grass seed and bean bag porridge was almost more than she could bear.

Lunch was more grass seed and bean bag porridge, flattened down this time and fried into pancakes. There were two each, and by the time people had chewed their way through their first one they were only too pleased to donate their second to the relief expedition. They were packed with the baby rusks and a few left over sweets in a couple of rucksacks.

"Now we've got to think of a sledge," said Samuel.

They were back in their classroom when he said this, getting over their pancake lunch and trying to make up their minds to return to the frozen climate of the ice tunnel. Everyone's eyes roved round the room as he spoke, searching for something large enough and strong enough and flat enough to be made into a sledge. Everyone's gaze seemed to end at Miss Gilhoolie's desk.

It was a beautiful desk. Mr Bedwig had made it for her before he left, planing and polishing solid pine to the smoothness and glossiness of best quality butterscotch. It was the only desk in the school that did not wobble.

"Solid as a rock," Mr Bedwig had said proudly when he brought it up from the basement. "Brass screws and dovetail joints. Should last for ever!"

"We'll have to get the legs off," said Dougal McDougal. "Let's get it turned over!"

"I can't bear to chop up Miss Gilhoolie's desk," protested Madeline.

"It's by far the best thing in the school to make a sledge from," said Dougal.

"There's other desks."

"Not strong enough. We can't have a sledge that falls to pieces at the first bump. And anyway, we won't be chopping it up, we'll just be converting it."

"I still can't bear it."

"Think of something better then."

Madeline went down to the basement and put in a little work on the ice tunnel while she tried to think of something better.

"It's got to be done," said Dougal cheerfully, and as soon as Madeline was out of the way he raided the tool box, and with a saw and a chisel hacked short the desk legs. Then Samuel Moon overcame his scruples and suggested taking out the drawers and using their fronts to make a sort of snowplough arrangement to fix on one end.

"And we can pull it by the drawer handles," he said. "We can make a harness out of belts or something."

The snowplough was made with some difficulty and the help of several large nails, but it was finished in the end, and two belts

were borrowed and attached and then the whole thing was manoeuvred through the trapdoor and down to the basement.

When Kate saw it, wrote Simon in his diary that night, *she said Oh Dougal Darling! And other people said other things, some of them very rude, but Madeline did not say anything.*

When Madeline saw it she went away from Class 4b and into the snow tunnel. She was gone for quite a long time, and when she came back she said, "I've finished it."

There was an immediate stampede, and a few minutes later for the first time for nearly a week, Class 4b stood out in the open air.

CHAPTER SIX

The Journey North

Samuel Moon woke up very early the next morning with a muddled feeling of intense gloom. Something bad was about to happen, he was sure, but he could not think what. And then it came to him. This was the day when the relief expedition was to set out in search of help.

And one of the relief expedition is *me*, thought Samuel in despair.

He knew he had only himself to blame. After all, it had been he who discovered the book of Antarctic adventures and read it aloud to the class. He had become the Pudding Bag School Antarctic expert.

But I only ever meant to be the sort of expert who *read* about things, he thought.

Not the sort who did them!

Too late now, Samuel realised. The relief expedition had been thought of, and in a moment of madness he had said that he didn't mind going.

Samuel did what Kate did when she wanted to cheer them up. He crawled quietly out from under his share of the red velvet curtain and lit the beeswax candle. Then he crawled quietly back in again and tried to be brave.

Charlotte and Emma woke up together, as all their lives they had done everything together. Charlotte was to go, and Emma was to stay. Whatever happened in the next few days, whether to Emma left behind in the forgotten school, or to Charlotte on the journey north, nothing would be quite as bad as the fact that one was to go, and one was to stay.

The twins did not say a word to each other, but under the red velvet curtain their hands met together and squeezed.

Bagdemagus uncurled from a red velvet dream and some instinct seemed to tell him that this was the day when his new career as an animated compass would begin. He crept up the basement steps and fortified himself with a visit to the black and white mice.

Madeline opened her eyes and the dim golden light of the beeswax candle was shining all around her. Now that she had to leave it she realised for the first time what a lovely place the basement refuge had been.

"Nothing will ever be the same again," thought Madeline.

Kate woke up saying, "Dougal darling!" and Dougal woke up absolutely jubilant because this was the day when the adventure would begin.

There was no more peace once Dougal was awake. There was nothing but a helter-skelter rush to make sure that the expedition was well on its way before the dinner ladies could do anything to stop it.

They were quickly ready. The four warmest coats had already been chosen for the expedition members, together with gloves and hats and scarves. The two rucksacks of food were packed and waiting, and so was a third one full of spare gloves and hats. The fourth rucksack was carried by Charlotte. The day before, the mustard and cross plantation had been divided into two. The last rucksack held the section that was to supply the relief expedition. It was to travel in a small greenhouse-style arrangement, made from rulers and plastic bags by Charlotte and Emma the previous evening.

"Well, at least you haven't much to carry," remarked Samantha. "And you'll have practically nothing when you've eaten that little bit of food you've got. I wonder if Bagdemagus will really work as a compass cat."

"I'm sure he will," said Madeline, and this was proved a few minutes later when the sledge had been dragged through the tunnel and parked on the snow outside. Bagdemagus, coaxed with great difficulty from the top of the boiler and carried by force into the freezing air outside, pointed at once and most determinedly in the direction of home.

"Poor Bagdemagus!" said Samantha.

"Good Bagdemagus!" said Kate, determined to be cheerful. "That's one thing that's working all right already!"

Dougal's sledge was another thing that looked like being a success. The conversion of Miss Gilhoolie's desk had worked beautifully. Even laden with the flat pack igloo, sleeping bags and groundsheet it ran at a wonderful speed.

"That's because she always kept it so well polished," remarked Samantha. "She was very proud of it! I remember how pleased she was when Mr Bedwig finished making it."

"Shut up Samantha!" ordered Dougal, seeing Madeline's stricken face at this tactless remark. "We had to chop it up! It was a matter of life or death! Anyway, it's just as much use as a sledge as it ever was as a desk!"

"That bit you and me hammered on the front makes a jolly good snow plough," observed Samuel. "And that lovely curvey bit Mr Bedwig put around the top was just right for runners when we sawed it up."

"Perhaps one day Mr Bedwig will be able

to turn it back into a desk again," said Madeline hopefully.

"If he can get the nails out," said Samantha.

"Shut *up*, Samantha darling!" said Kate. "Oh, I do wish they didn't have to go! Oh, take no notice of me! I'm sure everything is going to be absolutely all right!"

After that there was a lot of stamping of cold feet and blowing on of cold fingers and last minute chat about mustard and cress and dinner ladies and not eating Samantha, and everyone said how lucky it was that the snow seemed to have stopped for a while. And then everyone seemed to run out of words. Kate did quite a lot of hugging but nobody cried. Quite suddenly the relief expedition had begun.

They seemed to get far away very quickly, plodding steadily in the direction that everyone agreed looked most like north, over the strange snow-covered landscape of hillocks and bumps that was all that was left of Pudding Bag Lane. They turned around once to wave to those left behind, but that was all. Nobody looked back after that except Bagdemagus.

"I wonder if we'll ever see them again," said Samantha mournfully.

"Breakfast!" exclaimed Kate all at once, and began hurrying people back into the snow tunnel to go and get ready. Most of them went straight away, shivering and slipping and quite glad to get indoors, but Kate and Emma and Simon remained outside. They watched until their feet froze and their eyes streamed with rubbing and staring and rubbing again. They watched until the relief expedition were the size of ants, and the sledge was the size of a dot. And then, between one moment and another they seemed to disappear completely, but Kate and Emma and Simon still watched. And they stood very close together and they did not say a word.

Early mornings were the worst times of all for the dinner ladies. In the early mornings they never bothered to address each other as "Dame", and the time when they would be rescued and rewarded for all their hard work seemed very far away. Also they were beginning to run out of all but the plainest of biscuits, and they were getting rather tired of the meals they hotted up for themselves from the bottom of the Emergency Freezer. Not tired enough, of course, for them to think of eating their own cooking instead.

"But we still have to smell it," grumbled Mrs Muldoon as she stirred the morning saucepanful of grass seed and bean bag porridge.

"The fumes seemed to haunt me all night," agreed Amelia Pilchard. "I dreamed of old dogs!"

Mrs Muldoon and Miss Spigot looked most put out. Miss Pilchard was supposed to dream of much more glamorous things than old dogs.

"And what were the old dogs doing, Amelia dear?" asked Mrs Muldoon nastily.

"Panting," said Miss Pilchard. "Pass the plates, Pansy, do! Don't just stand there mooning!"

Miss Spigot, instead of passing the plates, marched angrily out of the kitchen and slammed the door. A few moments later however, she marched back in again, and there was a sort of awful triumph in her voice as she spoke.

"Four kiddies short!" she announced. "Four kiddies short! Dug a tunnel and hopped it! That Kate stood there and told me without turning a hair! Whatever shall we do?"

It took some time for her words to sink in. And then they had to rush out and check that they were true. And then they had to wring from Kate the whole story of the sledge and the escape tunnel and all the other preparations that had gone on under their hard-working and self-sacrificing noses. And then they had to tell Class 4b what they thought of their wicked, devious, ungrateful ways. This took a long time, so that breakfast, when it finally arrived, was very cold and gluey and stuck to the spoons quite horribly. It was well into the morning before the poor dinner ladies could sit down and catch their lost tempers and wonder together if Damehoods for outstanding nobleness in times of snow would be given to dinner ladies who had lost four children during the time that the outstanding nobleness took place.

They drank many cups of tea, and pondered the matter most dismally for most of the morning. And then they decided to blame Kate.

The reason that the relief expedition disappeared so suddenly and completely from sight was that they sank. The snow looked perfectly solid, but it was not. The snowdrifts had piled and frozen and piled again, but there were air pockets among them, especially around the drifted-over trees. At the end of Pudding Bag Lane the relief expedition plunged seven metres into the arms of an enormous chestnut tree.

Nobody was seriously damaged, but it took them most of the morning to clamber back up the snowy branches and out through the topmost twigs into the open air.

"We can't keep doing this," said Charlotte, anxiously inspecting the mustard and cress. "Some of the stalks have got terribly bent, and anyway, it hurts!"

"Let's build the igloo and have a rusk," suggested Dougal, but Madeline said they

could not possibly make their first camp at the end of Pudding Bag Lane, and Charlotte and Samuel agreed. "We've hardly started," said Samuel. "It must be miles and miles yet to the sunny north. Put Bagdemagus back on the sledge, and let's get on."

But Bagdemagus would not get back on the sledge. They had to unpack one of the igloo boxes in the end, and put him in that. And then he was no use at all as an animated compass, because he went round and round in circles, yowling with fury. However they plodded on, and shortly afterwards fell into another air pocket. After this Bagdemagus would not even go near the sledge. He set off in his own direction, and they had no choice but to follow him, because had they gone in the opposite direction, as originally planned, they would have lost him completely. Madeline hoped very much that he was not taking them in a circular direction back to Pudding Bag School, but she kept this thought to herself.

"One thing about following Bagdemagus," remarked Dougal an hour or so later.

"We've stopped falling down holes."

It was Madeline and Charlotte's turn to pull the sledge. They grunted, but did not reply. It was beginning to feel very heavy, and the sky was turning a darker and darker blue. Presently they saw a star, and then another, and then Madeline and Samuel made out the Great Bear and Pole star and saw to their relief that they were still going northish, if not absolutely straight north. Bagdemagus continued to stalk on ahead, making wide loops and detours from time to time, always well within sight, but also carefully out of reach. Everyone grew more and more tired.

Another hour passed, and Dougal and Samuel took over the towing. Bagdemagus still would not let himself be caught and Charlotte, despite herself, asked plaintively, "Are we nearly there?"

Bagdemagus carried on for a few further yards and then stopped.

They built their shelter by moonlight and starlight, scooping snow into the boxes with frozen hands. As soon as a box was filled and closed by one expedition member, it was

seized by another and added to the dome-shaped igloo. A third expedition member was kept busy filling in cracks and cementing the boxes together with snow. Last of all the sledge was lifted on top to close the final gap in the roof. It was not until the sledge was in place and packed down firmly with snowballs that Bagdemagus finally trusted them enough to return.

Inside the igloo it was black dark. Nobody cared. They spread out the groundsheet, pulled off their boots, unrolled their sleeping bags, crawled inside and collapsed.

"What about supper?" asked Dougal, after a long, long silence, but no one replied. Dougal fumbled a grass seed and bean bag pancake out of the knapsack that he was using for a pillow, took one bite, and fell asleep in mid-chew.

In Pudding Bag School nobody slept anything like so well. For one thing, they were terribly worried. The relief expedition had set out, and with nothing left to plan for, their thoughts turned more and more to the awfulness of their situation. Also, the shortness of the red velvet curtains with so much chopped off their ends to make sleeping bags was very much felt. People were continually becoming untucked, and this was not restful. Also, and worst of all, Miss Spigot was now sleeping down in the basement with them to ensure that no more people escaped. Class 4b discovered that Miss Spigot's disagreeable method of soothing herself to sleep was to pull her finger joints until they cracked. There was nobody in the basement that night who did not envy the relief expedition in their cardboard igloo in the snow.

The relief expedition woke up to find that they had camped in the shelter of an enormous, snow-covered dome. When they crawled out of the igloo and stamped their feet a strange whispering, ringing filled the air. They were all four of them enormously happy. The igloo had worked perfectly and their sleeping bags had been more comfortable than any beds they had ever known. They had survived a night, and the sky was bright blue and Charlotte said the mustard and cress had grown in the dark.

"Let's climb up to the top of that hill and see if we can see where we are," suggested Dougal.

Everyone looked at Bagdemagus to see whether this would be allowed, since it was becoming quite clear that he was the real leader of the expedition. Bagdemagus obviously thought it was a reasonable idea, he led the way quite cheerfully, and the hill seemed to whisper under their feet as they climbed.

Something was glinting on the top of the hill. They dug around, and found a gold cross and then Madeline exclaimed, "It's the dome of St Paul's!"

And it was.

They ate their pancake breakfast on the top of St Paul's Cathedral, and far away to their left Admiral Nelson kept them company. His column had almost disappeared, it was now a rather short stump, but they were pleased to see that the snowdrift behind it curved exactly like the prow of an enormous ship.

"He looks like the figurehead," said Samuel, with his mouth full of pancake.

After breakfast they sledged several times down the dome of St Paul's, because, as Dougal remarked, they would probably never get another chance. Then Bagdemagus took control again, leading them between half-buried, deserted office blocks and across empty spaces that he skirted with care. They ate baby rusks for lunch as they walked and consumed endless handfuls of snow to quench their thirst.

Gradually the cheerfulness of the early morning began to wear off. It was very hard going, Bagdemagus saved them from the snow pockets but he could not save them from everything. In some places the snow was so shallow that they stumbled over street lamps, and in others they found themselves skidding on the skylights of buildings buried beneath them. Dougal fell over a radio aerial and hurt his wrist. The sky changed from blue to white, and from white to grey, and from grey to yellowish brown, and then suddenly it was snowing very hard indeed.

They hardly had to work to fill the boxes for the igloo that night. They almost filled themselves. Everyone was covered in snow very quickly and the snow came with them when they crawled inside. There it melted, and the groundsheet soon became an icy puddle. There was no lying down that night. They sat back to back dozing miserably and chewing on pancakes. The air grew stuffy and then stale and suffocating.

"We're being buried," said Samuel and they realised this was true. Bagdemagus heroically crawled out through the entrance hole and clawed a tunnel up to the surface and this, while saving their lives, created such a horrible draught that they all privately thought it was not worth it.

"If we've got to go all the way to Scotland," said Charlotte, "I don't think I can bear it."

Already sledging on the dome of St Paul's seemed a very long time ago.

CHAPTER SEVEN

Howling in the Distance

Each day seems longer than the one before, wrote Simon Percy in his diary.

At Pudding Bag School the waiting was beginning to wear people down. They had not realised, when they planned the relief expedition, how much they would miss them when they were gone.

"I realised," said Emma. "I realised about Charlotte. Not about Samuel and Dougal and Madeline though."

Simon, in an effort to replace Samuel, had tried reading aloud Antarctic adventures to Class 4b at night. Somehow, it had not been the same at all.

"I'm sorry, Simon," said Kate. "But it doesn't seem to matter any more.

Dougal and Madeline were terribly missed, natural leaders that they were, and so was Bagdemagus. Even the dinner ladies missed Bagdemagus.

"There was a good two meals on that cat!" said Amelia Pilchard mournfully. "A good two meals *and* stock for soup! And it's walked off into the snow!"

"Try not to take it to heart, Amelia dear," said Mrs Muldoon kindly.

"*And* someone's been at the black-and-white mice," Miss Pilchard continued. "Three left there are, and the three thinnest ones too!"

"Have another Fondant Fancy," suggested Mrs Muldoon. "And try and remember the visions you saw. The statues and the flowers and crowds, and us on the telly!"

Amelia Pilchard sniffed and sighed.

"Amelia's right to be upset," said Miss Spigot, who had been rummaging in the Emergency Freezer while they talked. "I never thought to see the day when the tapioca would run out, and yet run out it has. And the grass seed and beans are just about gone.

We'll be down to Rock Bottom before the day's out, which I may as well tell you is Turkey Burgers and Pop Tarts and a burst bag of peas."

"Pansy dear, you cannot mean it!" exclaimed Mrs Muldoon, hastily eating the last Fondant Fancy.

"Lacie dear, I'm afraid it's true," said Miss Spigot.

One Bean soup for dinner, wrote Simon in his diary that day. *"One Bean soup means you get one bean each, so it wasn't exactly filling but we had mustard and cress for pudding which was very nice indeed*.

He underlined the last sentence and pushed his diary across the table for Emma to read because Kate said Emma needed cheering up. She had been terribly worried by the snowstorm that had begun the night before and she looked up nervously as Kate came in from another session of solar panel clearing on the roof.

"Stopped at last!" said Kate. "Cheer up

Emma! Now perhaps everything will start to come all right!"

The relief expedition knew that the snow had stopped when Bagdemagus disappeared through his ventilation tunnel and did not come back. One by one they followed after him, scrambling with cramped arms and legs through the new fall of snow. They found him sitting on a snowdrift, tidying his whiskers. As soon as he saw them he got up and stretched himself impatiently, as if just about to go.

"You'll have to wait while we dig our things out," Madeline told him, and he prowled irritably around them while they excavated first for the sledge and the igloo boxes, and then for their sleeping bags, rucksacks and groundsheet. As soon as they were properly loaded, he was off.

"He seems to know which way he wants to go," observed Charlotte. "I don't know how he can tell. Everything looks exactly the same to me. Do you want to know what I heard last night but I didn't like to tell you in case I frightened you?"

"What?" asked Dougal.

"Howling."

"*What?*"

"Howling like wolves. Far away wolves."

"I expect it was the wind," said Madeline, and Dougal and Samuel agreed.

"Wolves," said Charlotte stubbornly. "I was really worried about the mustard and cress. Where's Bagdemagus?"

Bagdemagus was far away to their left, a small orange dot in the snow.

"He's definitely taking us somewhere," said Madeline. "I'm sure he is. He's . . ."

She broke off suddenly, and looked at Charlotte.

"I told you so!" said Charlotte. "Howling!"

It was far, far away, the first sound of life they had heard since they left Pudding Bag School. It caused their hearts to beat faster and their skins to prickle all over with fear.

"Wolves," said Charlotte, and this time nobody disagreed.

Bagdemagus waited until he was sure that they had seen him, and set off again, and there was nothing they could do but follow.

Something was becoming more and more apparent as they journeyed. The snow was getting less deep. The drifts that had been piled to the height of St Paul's Cathedral were already behind them. It was like travelling from a landscape of snow-peaked mountains, into a country of rolling hills.

"It's hardly as high as the street lamps round here," said Dougal, as if snow as high as street lamps was hardly worth calling snow at all.

"It's still over the doors," said Charlotte, glancing at the buildings on either side. The buildings might as well have been blocks of ice, she thought, for all the use they were, blank-faced and silent and buried to their upper windows.

"The doors would probably be locked anyway," said Madeline, and everyone sighed, because something else besides the change in the depth of the snow was becoming very obvious. They were travelling in the direction of the wolves.

"I hope Bagdemagus is on *our* side!" said Charlotte suddenly. "After all, we don't know that he is!"

"Of course he is," said Madeline after a moment's startled silence. "He always has been, hasn't he?"

"*I* don't know," said Charlotte. "He wasn't very nice about us eating his cat food, was he? And he wouldn't sit on the sledge and be a proper compass cat when we needed him to. And now he's taking us in the direction of wolves!"

"Perhaps there's wolves in all directions," suggested Samuel. That was not a very comforting thought either.

"Perhaps he's not taking us anywhere at all," said Dougal. "After all, he's just a cat. Perhaps he's just wandering about, like cats do."

"He's not just any old cat!" cried Madeline hotly. "He's special! He's Bagdemagus!"

They paused and looked at Bagdemagus. He was perched on an old brick chimney stack vigorously licking his back end.

"He looks like any old cat to me," said Charlotte sadly.

As the light was fading they left the streets behind them and came into an open place of hills and hummocks and half-buried trees.

Bagdemagus stayed closer now, watching with gleaming eyes and twitching tail as they stumbled and tripped, and each time more slowly, clambered back to their feet.

"We ought to be thinking about camping for the night," said Madeline, and at that moment the howling, which they had not heard for some time, broke out directly in front of them, and very close indeed.

Charlotte sobbed, and Dougal exclaimed, "Look at Bagdemagus! I'm beginning to *hate* Bagdemagus! He's pleased! He's brought us here on purpose and he's pleased!"

Dougal was right, Bagdemagus, springing jauntily ahead of them as if hurrying to greet the hidden wolves, looked very pleased indeed. He disappeared over a ridge of snow, and the wolf voices sang louder than ever.

"He's not on our side after all," said Samuel fearfully, but Madeline shouted, "Look!"

Bagdemagus came bounding back with twelve wolves behind him and everyone sighed with enormous relief because the twelve wolves were in double file and harnessed to a sleigh.

"It's Mr Bedwig!" said Madeline, and it was.

Mr Bedwig was short and fat with white hair and spectacles. He looked exactly the sort of person who would spend a hard winter dozing in front of a fire with a crossword puzzle. But Mr Bedwig had hidden talents, and school caretaking and rocket building were just the beginning of them. His ancestors had been caretakers in the Ark, he had often told Class 4b in the past, and handiness with animals ran in his family. So did coping with emergencies without any fuss and not being upset by a bit of weather. There was no one in the world, thought Madeline, quite like Mr Bedwig. There was no one in the world she would rather have met just then.

"Now then Madeline Brown and Co." said Mr Bedwig, bringing his wolf team and sleigh to a tidy halt as he spoke. "Whatever have you been up to with that poor old cat of mine?"

The relief expedition rushed to explain.

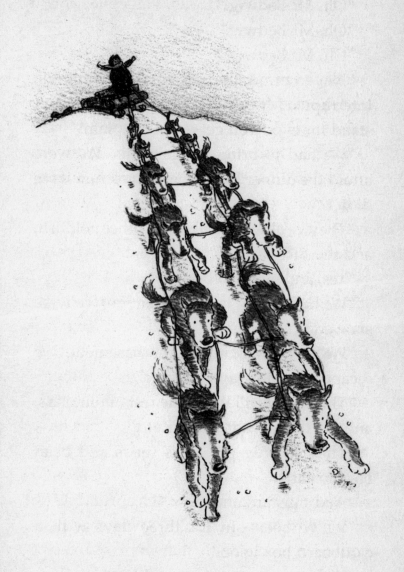

"Oh, Mr Bedwig!"

"Oh, Mr Bedwig!"

"Oh, Mr Bedwig!"

"Never mind the Oh Mr Bedwigging!" interrupted Mr Bedwig. "These wolves won't stand for ever! You get on and explain!"

"We had to bring Bagdemagus. We were afraid the dinner ladies might cook him if we didn't."

"They've already cooked the office goldfish, and the stick insects."

"Yes, and gerbil kebabs!"

"We had dinner ladies' detention; we were snowed up for days!"

"We've been living in the basement. We escaped through your passage."

"They're all still there, the rest of our class, and the dinner ladies and Kate."

"They've only got grass seeds and bean bags to eat."

"And mustard and cress."

"We've been out for three days with a cardboard box igloo."

"We dug a huge tunnel and Kate made us sleeping bags."

"Bagdemagus was a compass cat. He brought us to you."

"We're terribly, terribly sorry about Miss Gilhoolie's desk."

"Well I never!" said Mr Bedwig, seeming to be quite bowled over by this flood of information. "Well I never, never did! Clever old Puss! And now I think the lot of you had best come back with me."

"Back where?" asked Dougal, Samantha and Samuel, but Madeline knew the answer already. Kate had told them long ago. Mr Bedwig had been left in charge of the cold weather animals. They were going back to the zoo.

There was room on the sleigh for everyone and the sledge (at which Mr Bedwig tutted but made no comment) tied on behind. "Now no pushing or loud talk," he warned. "I've got the reindeer trained to pull as gentle as lambs but these are pure bred Siberian wolves and they excite very easy!"

Charlotte clutched Bagdemagus tightly at this remark.

"They haven't been getting the exercise they

should," explained Mr Bedwig. "What with having to take turns with the reindeer and moose! And I can't turn them loose on account of the penguins . . ."

Samuel gave a huge yawn and suddenly nodded forward.

"Not to mention the polars who've no patience at all . . ."

As patient as polars, thought Madeline drowsily. On account of the penguins . . . Pure bred Siberian . . . don't get the exercise . . .

Madeline was asleep and Samuel was asleep. Charlotte's head tipped further and further forward until it came to rest on Bagdemagus's furry gold coat, and it was like tilting into a dream. Dougal, swaying from side to side with the motion of the sleigh said, "I'm jolly well not . . . going to sleep . . . like they have . . ." and came to rest against Mr Bedwig's broad shoulder and did not speak again.

Mr Bedwig's winter quarters were the old Keeper's Lodge of the zoo. From there he had constructed a series of ice tunnels leading in all directions, to the penguins' frozen lake, the wolf dens, the reindeer stables and polar bear enclosure, all buried under the snow. Further tunnels led to the surface, so that the animals could be properly exercised and to the zoo warehouses, where vast supplies of food, both human and animal were stored away.

"A place for everything and everything in it's place," remarked Mr Bedwig as he unloaded his sleeping passengers at the Keeper's Lodge and drove the wolf team away to be rubbed down and fed.

In the Keeper's Lodge the relief expedition slept and slept. Ages and ages later they woke up to the smell of sausages and baked potatoes, and found themselves tucked up in a tidy line on the floor with rugs and cushions. Through an open door they could see Mr Bedwig lifting dishes from an oven and carrying them to a table, sausages, baked potatoes, rice pudding and apple pie.

"How long have we been asleep?" asked Madeline.

"Round the clock," said Mr Bedwig. "And

half-way round the clock again! I don't know what you might call this meal, breakfast or supper, but it's ready when you are!" And he plonked a jug of hot chocolate in the middle of the table.

Madeline, Dougal, Samuel and Samantha looked at the hot chocolate. Then they looked at each other, and they thought of Kate and Simon and all their friends eating grass seed and bean bag porridge in the gloomy dining room of Pudding Bag School, and Madeline said, "Mr Bedwig, do you think it would keep hot?"

At supper time Kate said that she was not hungry, and Mrs Muldoon said, "Suit yourself," and Kate went out on to the roof.

It was nearly dark, but no stars shone. A tear trickled down Kate's nose as she thought of the supper going on in the school below, cold bean salad and grass seed soup. Another tear fell as she remembered the anxious face of Emma as she bent over the last of the mustard and cress, and then a whole shower of tears for Dougal, Madeline, Samuel and Charlotte far away in the snow. And then, on the wind, came a sound that stopped Kate's tears like magic. Sleigh bells. Sleigh bells coming closer and closer.

The journey that had taken the relief expedition so long was retraced in less than an hour. Mr Bedwig and Bagdemagus led the way with the wolf sleigh, and Charlotte and Dougal followed behind driving nine reindeer and a moose.

"Can't take you all," Mr Bedwig had warned, and Samuel and Madeline, thinking of how anxious Kate and Emma must be and realising that extra sausages and potatoes would be needed, had nobly volunteered to stay behind and cook.

Once again they steered by Bagdemagus, but this time he rode instead of marching ahead, and all the way his nose pointed unwaveringly in the direction of home. They passed out of the empty park and through the silent streets in minutes, skirted the dome of St Paul's and headed due south to Pudding

Bag Lane and Kate, standing among the snowy roofpeaks with tears drying on her cheeks.

CHAPTER EIGHT

What Happened In The End

The sound of the sleigh bells, mingled with Kate's shrieks of joy, penetrated down to the dining room where Class 4b were gathered.

In no time at all the room was empty. They raced through the classrooms and down to the basement, tore along the passage and burst out of the tunnel into the open air. Then for a few minutes there was a most joyful reunion in the snow.

"You'll catch your deaths-a-cold," said Mr Bedwig in the end, when the hugging and exclaiming showed signs of diminishing and Samantha had stopped saying over and over again that she never thought they could still be alive. "Go and wrap up warm and come straight back! No you can't stroke the doggies,

Young Lady! They are pure-bred Siberian wolves and excite very easy! Hurry up the lot of you! And don't forget those blessed dinner ladies that I've heard so much about!"

They were ready in a very few minutes, and they did not forget the dinner ladies, who came over "All sudden jelly" as Mrs Muldoon put it, at the news of rescue at last. The guinea pigs, gerbils and black-and-white mice were stowed in Mr Bedwig's pockets and the two sleighs were packed.

"A tight squeeze," remarked Mr Bedwig.

"But I daresay it would have been tighter a week ago. Anyway, we'll soon have you there."

"Dougal darling," said Kate, a little while later. "Ought you to drive so very, very fast?"

"Yes I ought," replied Dougal, slapping the reins up and down vigorously as he spoke. "Madeline and Samuel are cooking supper. Sausages, baked potatoes, rice pudding and apple pie!"

"He's a very gallant old gent!" said Mrs Muldoon, a day or two later, and she smiled patronisingly at Mr Bedwig's back as he disappeared down one of the snow tunnels that connected the buildings at the zoo.

Miss Spigot and Miss Pilchard nodded in kindly agreement, because there was no denying Mr Bedwig's gallantry. He had rescued them when they were down to their last three turkey burgers and had almost lost all hope. He had given up the Keeper's Lodge for them and moved uncomplainingly into the monkey house instead. He had taken over responsibility for Class 4b, and last, and best of all, he refused to allow them to cook. He said they had done enough and the dinner ladies quite agreed.

Class 4b were also living in the monkey house, two or three to a cage and very comfortable indeed. They spent their time helping to take care of the cold weather animals (fourteen wolves, nine reindeer, one moose, two polar bears and forty-two penguins) and learning to cook. The time passed very quickly and happily and there was great disappointment when the Great Thaw arrived and the snow tunnels linking the cages began to collapse and green grass appeared for the first time in weeks.

The Great Thaw was followed by South West Gales and a heatwave which was very useful because it meant that the melting snowdrifts disappeared almost instantly instead of causing floods. In a remarkably short period of time London was back to normal again, and Class 4b were restored to their loving families, who all the time had believed them to be living happily in a remote

Scottish castle, not bothering to write.

And so Class 4b, Pudding Bag School, returned to its usual quiet life, but the dinner ladies did not. The story of their nobleness moved the nation, and they were given Damehoods and lifelong pensions and featured in a documentary on Prime Time TV. They never went back to cooking. Dame Amelia became a fortune teller and Dame Lacie a chat show host and Dame Pansy wrote a best selling book called *COPING WITH THE KIDDIES* which was later filmed. White marble statues were erected to all three of them in Regent's Park and Pudding Bag School had a day off for the unveiling.

There were crowds and cheering and thousands of flowers, wrote Simon Percy in his diary that night. *But they none of them seemed surprised.*

At Pudding Bag School the missing stick insects and gerbils and black-and-white mice were soon replaced, and Mr Bedwig repaired Miss Gilhoolie's desk so that it was as good as new. Bagdemagus continued to live with them, spending most of his days asleep in patches of sunlight, but always waking in time to share the packed lunches that people now brought instead of school dinners.

"He's a very good cat," said Dougal McDougal.

"He's the best in the world," said Madeline Brown.